The FOREVER FRIENDS CLUB

by Sue Gainor
and Sarah P. Gibson
Illustrated by Miranda R. Mueller

drt press
books for families

The Forever Friends Club

Attention non-profits and corporations: quantity discounts available for fundraisers and gifts. Please contact us!

Published by:
DRT Press
PO Box 427
Pittsboro, NC 27312
Tel: (919)360-7073; Fax (866)562-5040
www.drtpress.com

Written by Sue Gainor and Sarah P. Gibson
Illustrated by Miranda R. Mueller http://www.mirandarmueller.com/
Illlustrations in prismacolor and ink on Strathmore Recycled Artagain paper.
Designed by Jeffrey Duckworth http://www.duckofalltrades.com/
Printed in China.

10 9 8 7 6 5 4 3 2
Publisher's Cataloging-in-Publication data

Gainor, Sue.
    The forever friends club / Sue Gainor and Sarah Gibson ; illustrated by Miranda R. Mueller.
        p. cm.
    Summary: Four best friends form a club for adopted children; the only problem is that Sam isn't adopted. To help Sam feel like he belongs, the friends "adopt" him into their Forever Friends club.
    ISBN 978-1-933084-02-2
[1. Adoption--Fiction. 2. Intercountry adoption--Fiction. 3. Families --Fiction. 4. Friends—Fiction.] I. Gibson, Sarah P., 1962- II. Mueller, Miranda R. III. Title.

PZ7.G1285 Fo 2010
[E]—dc22   2009939192

Thanks to our friends: Elly Blue, Riana, Emerson, Vanessa, Oscar, and Monica! You were a huge help!

This book is for all the Forever Families.

Table of Contents

1.
New Neighbors

Sam Trudeau lived on Oak
Street.
He had a Mom, a Dad,
and a dog named Buck.
Life was good, but sometimes
he wished for a friend
to play with.
Then Madison moved in next
door…

Madison called herself a
CREE-AY-TOR.

She created a *Leaning Castle*
in his sandbox.

She created a *Heap of Toys*
in his room.

She created a *Moosh*
at lunch made of:

peanut butter,
carrot sticks,
jelly,
bread,
and potato chips.
(She called it a masterpiece
but she did not get dessert).

Madison created her way
into Sam's life and
'things' were never quite
the same again.

Then Nikolai's family bought
the house across the street.
Nick rocked!
All the time.
He swung,
he rolled,
he skipped,
he twirled,
and he hopped,
from the moment he woke up
to the moment he went to bed.
Even during quiet time
he rocked and rocked.
Sam and Madison became
so used to the movement
they forgot Nick was doing it.

5

Isabel arrived one day,
in the middle of summer,
when they were all seven.
She marched into Madison's yard
on a Thursday afternoon and
commanded, "Let's have fun!"

She knew lots of exciting games:

tag,
kickball,
sardines,
red rover,
hide and seek
capture the flag,
duck, duck, goose,
red light-green light...

7

They laughed, and ran,
and shouted.
Until they were all sweaty,
and hot, and out-of-breath.
Then Isabel went home
to plan more games.
Nick went home
too exhausted to rock.
Madison went home
too tired to create.

And Sam went home,
too full of friends to wish
for any more

2.
The Playhouse

It rained the next day.
Nick's Mom shooed them
into the playroom.

There, Isabel directed:
pillow fights (until ordered to stop),
play dough animal making,
standing on head contests,
paper-airplane flying,
couch fort-building,
thumb wrestling,
hide the button,
Simon says...

Until they all collapsed
on the floor.
Even Nick sat still.

Isabel then quizzed them.
She quickly found out
their birthdays and
their favorite colors.
She also discovered that
they were adopted:
Isabel from Guatemala,
Nick from Russia, and
Madison from Wisconsin.
Except for Sam.
He had one set of parents
and was from Oak Street
only.
He felt a little left out.
It made him sad.

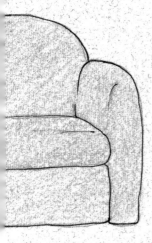

When Sam came home
he asked his Mom,
"Did I grow in your tummy?"
"Oh, yes," Mom smiled,
"Right below my heart."

"Did you see me born?"
he asked his Dad.
"I was the first one to hold you!"
Dad beamed.
Sam sighed.
They were nice answers.
But they didn't make him
feel better.

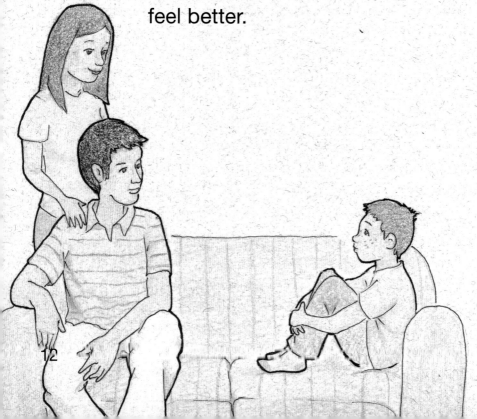

The following week,
Isabel discovered the old
tool shed.
It sat in the far back
of Madison's yard.
"It's perfect!" she declared.
She marched inside to ask
Madison's mom if they
could use it.

Then she and
Madison lugged out
empty boxes. Sam
picked up the trash.
Nick swept the floor,
back and forth.

Madison's Mom let them use
an old table and four chairs.
Plus they found a rickety
rocking chair in the basement.
Nick dragged it into a corner
of the shed and rocked.
The other three sat down
at the table.

"It's a *marvelous* playhouse!"
Madison cried, flinging her
arms into the air.
"It's not a playhouse!" Isabel said.
"It's not?"
"It's a clubhouse—for meetings
of our club," Isabel announced
importantly.
"What club?" Sam asked.
Nick stopped rocking to listen.

3.
Naming the Club

"*Our* club," Isabel said.
"And we need a name for it—something that is about *us*."
"The Seven Club?" Madison said.
"But what happens when one of us turns eight?" Sam pointed out.
"The Adopted Club?" Madison tried again.

"I have a forever family,"
Nick said from the corner.
"What's a forever family?"
Sam asked.
"It's another name for an adoptive family.
We choose to belong
together forever," Madison
explained. "Hey, I know! We could
be *The Forever Friends Club*."

Isabel nodded slowly.
 "I like it!" she declared.
 Nick said, "But Sam's not
adopted."
Everyone looked at Sam,
who looked at the floor.
"That's okay, he can still
belong," Isabel said with
a wave of her hand.
Then she and Madison
began to argue.

Isabel wanted to write the
club rules.
Madison insisted they had to
paint the walls first.
"Blue!" Nick called out.
"I don't want to be in your
stupid club," Sam said.
Isabel stopped waving.
Madison stopped arguing.
Nick stood up.
But they didn't follow Sam
when he stomped outside.

19

The next day Sam stayed home
and played by himself.
It was quiet.
It was lonely.
He hugged Buck.
He loved him, and Mom and Dad.
He didn't want a different family.
But he did want to belong
to The Forever Friends Club.

Outside his window he could
see Isabel and Madison.
They were playing in Isabel's sandbox.
Nick was swinging on the
swing set beside them.
Sam sighed.
He wanted to ask them
if they would still play
with him anyway.
But he was afraid.
What if they said no?

Sam went outside and
walked slowly across the lawn.
He stopped at the gate.
He took a deep breath.
Isabel looked up and saw him.
"Sam!" she cried.
She and Madison and Nick
ran to open the gate.
Before Sam could speak,
Isabel said, "Please join
the club! *We* will adopt you
and then you can be a member."
Nick hopped up and down.
"Your forever friends!" he said.
Madison added, "Come on!
It will be fun!"

Happiness spread from Sam's
heart out to his fingertips.
He wanted to shout.
He wanted to jump.
However, all he did was nod
because he couldn't find
the words.
It didn't matter.
His friends understood.

4.
A Book for Sam

They led him to the clubhouse.
Three books lay on the table.
"These are our Life Stories,"
Isabel said.

Then she pulled a another book
out of a bag.
Isabel showed it to Sam:

Sam opened his book
to the first page:

adoshen apleashen
Name: Sam Trudeau
Date: Augest 24

Brith Pairents: Mike and leanne

Adopetev friends: Madison, Nick, Isabel

Qushen 1: Are you a nice person?

Nick: Yes I am!

Madison: Yes and an artest too

Isabel: Very nice!

Qushen 2: Why do you wish to adopet Sam?

Nick: Sam is god at basball

Madison: Sam shars his toys

Isabel: Sam folows derexshons

Qushen 3: Will you be a forever friend?

Nick: Yes!

Madison: Yes!!

Isabel: YES!!!

27

Isabel took out a piggybank.
"My Mom says you have to
pay and do the paperwork,"
she explained.
Nick, Madison, and Isabel
each

dropped a quarter
into the piggybank.
"Now we have visits
to decide whether we
are right for each other,"
Isabel said.
Everyone stared at Sam,
who stuttered, "I...I..."

"Enough visiting!" Isabel
interrupted. "I vote we adopt him!"
Nick and Madison's hands
shot up into the air.
Isabel nodded. "Time to go see
the judge."
"How do *you* know?"
Madison demanded.

Isabel said, "Because I remember."
Nick stopped playing with
his book.
"You do?" Sam asked.
"I was four."
Isabel spoke quietly and
they all leaned in to hear.

"The judge was dressed in black,
and sat way up high above me.
He asked me if I would like to
choose to be part of a new family.
I told him...yes!"
"Wow," they all whispered.
Isabel stood up again.
This time they followed—
sure that she knew what she
was doing.

They walked around the shed
and then back inside.
Isabel pulled a black cape
out of her bag and handed it
to Madison.
 "You be the judge," she ordered.
"Nick and I will be the parents."

"*I* want to be the judge,"
Nick demanded.
"But you're the father!"
Isabel said.
Nick shrugged.
"You be the father," he said,
stubbornly crossing his arms.

Isabel rolled her eyes
up to the ceiling,
heaved a great sigh,
and handed the cape over.
Nick tied it on then
stepped up onto a chair.

Sam asked, "What are you doing?"
"Getting up high," Nick answered.
"No rocking on that chair!"
Isabel ordered.
Nick became as still as one
of Madison's sculptures
(which meant he was wobbling).

5.
Sam Speaks

Isabel cleared her throat.
She said in a loud, deep voice,
"We ask the judge to let
Madison, Isabel and Nick,
adopt Sam Trudeau.
We want to become
his forever friends."

There was a moment of silence.
"Say—*do you want to be adopted*?"
Isabel hissed at Nick.
"Do you want to be adopted?"
Nick quickly repeated.
"Did he?" Sam thought.

Sam looked at Nick
trying not to wobble the chair.
He looked at Madison
twirling her hair into a tangle.
He looked at Isabel
tapping her foot on the floor.

Well, each one was unique.
Sometimes they were fun.
And sometimes they were not.
But they were all willing
to be his friend.
And wasn't that what
he had wished for?

"YES!" Sam said.

"YOU ARE ADOPTED!"
Nick announced before Isabel
could say anything else.
Madison clapped.
Nick hopped down off the chair.
Isabel handed Nick a pen.
He carefully signed
Sam's adoption paper.

Then Isabel stamped it:

"And now Sam is a member
of *The Forever Friends Club*!"
Isabel announced.
Sam sighed in relief.
He was very happy
to be part of the club.
But being adopted
was a tiring process.
He was glad it was over.

Isabel packed away
the books,
the cape,
the stamp,
and the pen.
Then the four members of the club
sat down to eat cookies
and plan the rest of their day
together.